THE YOUNG FRONTIERSMAN Series - Book 1

FIDELITY

A Story of the Revolutionary War

I0546026

Matthew Blaine

MILFORD
HOUSE

an imprint of Sunbury Press, Inc.
Mechanicsburg, PA USA

MILFORD HOUSE

an imprint of Sunbury Press, Inc.
Mechanicsburg, PA USA

Copyright © 2024 by Matthew Blaine.
Cover Copyright © 2024 by Sunbury Press, Inc.

For information about special discounts for bulk purchases, please contact Sunbury Press Orders Dept. at (855) 338-8359 or orders@sunburypress.com.

To request one of our authors for speaking engagements or book signings, please contact Sunbury Press Publicity Dept. at publicity@sunburypress.com.

FIRST MILFORD HOUSE PRESS EDITION: March 2024

Set in Adobe Garamond Pro | Interior design by Crystal Devine | Cover by Lawrence Knorr | Edited by Lawrence Knorr.

Publisher's Cataloging-in-Publication Data
Names: Blaine, Matthew, author.
Title: Fidelity : a story of the Revolutionary War / Matthew Blaine.
Description: First trade paperback edition. | Mechanicsburg, PA : Milford House Press, 2024.
Summary: To defend Fort Ticonderoga in 1777, young courier Barnabas Locke serves as a spy on the border with Canada to track a pending British assault. He reunites with his Abenaki friend, makes an enemy of a British lieutenant, flees Huron warriors, and encounters another spy on the run. On the battlefield, he comes to the rescue of Benedict Arnold.
Identifiers: ISBN : 979-8-88819-187-3 (paperback).
Subjects: YOUNG ADULT FICTION / Action & Adventure / General | YOUNG ADULT FICTION / Historical / United States / Colonial & Revolutionary Periods | FICTION / Historical / Colonial America & Revolution.

Designed in the USA
0 1 1 2 3 5 8 13 21 34 55

For the Love of Books!

For my sister, Alane, who provided the tools.

CONTENTS

ACKNOWLEDGMENTS

Every storyteller needs trusted first readers to offer edits, suggestions, and criticisms that combined make the story being told smarter, sharper and more engaging. By good luck, the following volunteered their time and keen eyes to the task.

Jim Glenn
Denise Glenn
Stephen Balchunas
Jerry Treon

INTRODUCTION

IN SEPTEMBER, 2012, I was touring by automobile the Adirondack region of New York. A winding road along Lake George led me by happenstance to Fort Ticonderoga. I spent nearly half a day exploring on my own and, when available, leaning into small group tours. I very much appreciated the knowledge of the docents, the authenticity of the restoration, and the care and attention to period detail made by the handful of re-enactors who were on site that day. My mind went instantly into overdrive, creating characters and situations even before I knew the history of the fort itself and its role in the Revolutionary War. I tend to imagine myself as an unseen, unknown character whenever I walk the grounds of historic sites, for example, at Bandolier National Park in New Mexico or in Custer, a living museum at a restored gold mining town in Idaho. History really does come alive in such places and jolts my imagination into the realm of "what if." Fort Ticonderoga never left my imaginative subconscious.

After mining my personal history in two short collections of memoirs, the idea of writing a fictional story for adolescent readers about an adventurous youth (yes, an imagined youthful version of myself) occurred to me. And Fort Ticonderoga came back into focus: the realism of its atmosphere created by the restorers, the re-enactors and the docents. The day I visited was a quiet day at the Fort, and I had a few fellow tourists cluttering my photographs or imposing their 21st-century presence.

To understand the pivotal role of Fort Ticonderoga in the story you are about to read, you require some acquaintanceship with its history.

Fort Ticonderoga, a small stone star-shaped fort with five bastions, is located at the southern end of Lake Champlain in New York very near the Vermont border. Built by the French between 1755 and 1758, it changed hands several times between the British and the French during the French and Indian War and several times between the British and the Americans in the early years of the Revolutionary War. Its strategic importance lies in its control of the Hudson River Valley, the Mohawk Trail through New York, and the New Hampshire Grants (the upper region of the present states of New Hampshire and Vermont, then called Coos and hotly contested).

History provided the names of numerous generals. Quartermaster General Udney Hay, General

John "Gentleman Johnny" Burgoyne, and General Benedict Arnold are among those who figure in this story. All of the other characters are my own fiction, with the notable exception of Captain Benjamin Whitcomb, Jr. A legend in his own time for his scouting exploits during the French and Indian War, Captain Whitcomb usefully served as a model for the character of young Barnabas Locke. As for the Native Peoples, who had the most at stake throughout this period of turmoil and shifting allegiances, I did my best to make my Abenaki characters true to their period. I did sufficient research to set the characters in their place and time, but not always, in fact.

Special thanks for their inspiration to Fess Parker, Daniel Day-Lewis, Russell Means and Wes Studi, James Fenimore Cooper, Captain William Clark, Sacagawea, and her French husband, Toussaint Charbonneau.

Although written with young readers in mind, I hope their elders will also enjoy the story. As a disclaimer, I identify myself as a "storyteller," not as an expert or historian in any field. However, I have done due diligence in seeking authentic sources for information and inspiration.

Matthew Blaine
Storyteller
May 2022

ONE

THE HOURGLASS

The yellow-haired young man stumbled down a short bank onto the hard road behind them. The boys turned as one, each pulling a tomahawk from his belt. The running man did not pause as he passed them, but he did gasp the curious words: "Don't choose the roan. His heart is from Hell."

Barnabas and Ned Locke, cousins, watched the wet young man disappear down the road toward Green's Crossing, their destination. What in blazes was that all about, they wondered, and why was he soaking wet? The young man, with his strange message, furnished an interesting topic for speculation the rest of their way to the crossroads. They had heard that a recruiter there was signing up militiamen for a ranger company under the command of the famous Captain Benjamin Whitcomb. Son of a Vermont farmer, Ned was determined to serve his duty as a patriot. He hoped for a summer spent at arms and perhaps a return to the farm in time for the fall cider pressing.

His cousin Barnabas had a wilder nature, brought up in his dead father's fur trade with the Abenaki. The late Mr. Locke had been a canny and diplomatic trader with the "People of the Dawn Land," as the proud Abenaki called themselves. They were eager to trade their furs for English goods but had generally allied with the French on political matters. Barnabas had been well-schooled in both English trade practices and Indian wood lore. As an orphan, he understood that his own choices would henceforward dictate his future. At this age, what he knew best was being a free man of the frontier. Yet he wanted to support his cousin and friend Ned in this great adventure of war.

As they approached the crossroads, they scanned for a recruiting station. In a pasture just beyond the tavern, they spied milling men, a few in uniform, but most garbed in civilian buckskins and homespun linsey-woolsey. And leaning against a split rail was the yellow-haired young man, no longer running, in conversation with two soldiers, one with the red epaulet and stripes of a sergeant, the shorter with a corporal's stripe. As the wheezing young man followed the corporal away, he grinned at the two boys approaching the sergeant.

"Excuse me, Sir," Ned said. "My cousin and I look to sign up for the militia. Can you do that for us, Sir?" The sergeant took time to study Ned's ruddy face and sturdy stature and Barnabas's whiplash leanness. He took note of Barnabas's long dark hair clubbed behind his head right down to the well-greased moccasins on his feet. He stroked his stubbled chin, "Are you boys yet 17?"

"We are," they replied as one.

"Obliged to any term of servitude or married?"

"We are not! We are free men."

The sergeant nodded in consideration. He prided himself on his judgment of men. Turning to Ned, he said, "You'll do, son. You've got a steady look about you." Addressing Barnabas, he opined, "You, boy, you've got the look of a running man. But can you read?"

And Barnabas snapped back, "I never ran from any fight, Sir! And yes, my Ma, God bless her, learnt me Bible reading, and Pa taught me the value of a coin."

"I'm Sergeant Joshua. You don't call me 'sir.' You call an officer 'Sir.' Corporal Sharpe there," and he pointed his beefy thumb toward a table and chair in front of a tent, "will enlist you both, but you," and here he turned again to Barnabas, "you might make a runner if you want. The company needs running men to serve as couriers. But there's a test you have to pass first, not an easy one."

Barnabas felt the thrill of a challenge course through him, setting his feet afire. "I like a good long run. What do I have to do?"

"Run, lad, like the hounds of Hell are on your heels. By the by, can you ride a horse, saddled or bare?"

"I never been thrown yet."

Sergeant Joshua strode before them to the little table where Corporal Sharpe already had the muster rolls open. The sergeant took up an hourglass in his meaty hand and said, "If you can run a five-mile course—with some few obstacles along the way—and get back to me before I turn this glass, you might do. But if you can recite word for word the message that I whisper in your ear, then you're a running man. First, Corporal Sharpe here will record your enlistment as of second April 1777, as privates serving in Captain Benjamin Whitcomb's Independent Corps of Rangers."

But Barnabas was curious. "That young man I saw you talking to, is he a running man?"

"No, lad, he's a foot soldier now."

Standing shoulder to shoulder with his cousin as they signed their enlistment papers for a voluntary term of two years, Ned recognized that his cousin was already embarking on a different path. No one was as fast as Barnabas Locke, on a horse or on foot. He always went full gallop. Respectfully, Ned asked Sergeant Joshua, "May I remain to see if Barnabas here beats your hourglass?"

"You'll know that the next time you see him. Go with the Corporal, lad. He's already got another recruit waiting to get outfitted."

The sergeant led Barnabas to a stake with a wisp of blue cloth fluttering in the breeze. "From this start point, you have to navigate your way back to me before I turn the glass." Through the meadow grass, Barnabas saw the tracks of other runners headed toward the wood line. He spied a blue ribbon fluttering from a branch and figured that was the sign pointing to the path into the forest. Sergeant Joshua took a leather dispatch bag, weighted with sand, and draped it over Barnabas's lean shoulder. "And now I'm about to tell you the message that you must deliver word for word, a message that might cost the lives of your fellows should you fail." And he leaned over to whisper into Barnabas's ear words that made no sense at all. And then he turned the hourglass. "Run, boy, like the hounds are on your heels." And shoved him towards the woods. Barnabas heard his hoarse voice shouting after him, "Don't you lose one grain of my sand!"

Shadows were already lengthening across the pasture as Barnabas made a beeline for the blue ribbon and entered the tree line. Focussed on the task ahead, he repeated the strange message the sergeant had whispered in his ear. The more he repeated the message, the less sense it made. Maybe that was part of the test? "Even though it means naught to me, it must mean something. So, I'm not going to think about it, just repeat it in my mind from time to time. To keep it fixed."

The stony trail was narrow. Overhanging branches, newly budding, had been broken. Clearly, others had run this trail before him. Loose in his bones, nothing aching even though he had been on the move since just past dawn, he had fallen into an easy rhythm when he saw the forest path open ahead of him into a clearing. Standing in its midst, a man held two horses by their reins. The roan was saddled, but the smaller bay was not. The yellow-haired young man's message flashed into his mind. "Don't choose the roan. His heart is from Hell!"

Approaching at a run, Barnabas instantly made his choice. The man standing between the horses was signaling him towards the roan, throwing reins over the roan's neck. He stumbled backward, startled when Barnabas never paused but vaulted over the bay's round rump onto his bare back. The bay was startled, too. Barnabas seized the reins and a hank of mane and put his heels into the bay's sides.

A backward glance showed Barnabas the man struggling to regain control over the roan while the bay was already galloping out of the clearing and onto the path. It was a wild ride—down and up ravines, hurdling fallen trees. Barnabas hugged the bay with his legs and leaned into his neck. This horse knew his own soul, and it was not a black one from Hell. It was willing and brave.

Surely, it was at least a long mile when the path opened again into another clearing. This one held a makeshift empty corral with the gate open. An old fellow leaned against the railings. He straightened up quickly when Barnabas and the bay hurtled toward him. He raised a hand and shouted, "Where's the roan?" The bay, well-schooled, brought himself to a halt. As Barnabas dismounted, he whispered into the bay's ear the message Sergeant Joshua had entrusted to him. The bay flattened his ears and jerked his head up. To the old fellow, Barnabas replied, "Didn't think the roan would measure up." As he took the bay's reins, the old fellow chuckled and pointed the way into the dense woods. "You're back on your own two feet, laddy."

Running deeper into the forest, Barnabas sensed that he was dropping into cooler terrain. He began to hear the rumble of a fast-moving creek. He already felt cool water in his dry throat. The rumble soon turned into the muted roar of a creek running at full spring melt through boulders and deadfalls. He paused long enough on the bank to slake his thirst and then scanned up and down the fast water for a fording place. There was a tree—an old pine covered in slippery moss and bristling with dead, spiky branches. It rested mid-stream on a boulder, also slippery. From that point, it looked like a long jump onto a smaller rock within a few feet of the opposite bank. Is this how those other runners had crossed? A vision of the wet young man flashed into his mind. Footprints on a broken piece of the bank indicated where crossers had entered the icy spring melt-off. He knew instinctively that the creek was where most of the prospective runners had failed the challenge of the hourglass. The bank was broken, but the unscuffed log was still mossy. So be it. The log!

He jiggled the dead pine by jumping up and down on it, testing that it wouldn't break beneath him. His eyes charted each footstep and each handhold, making sure the leather pouch over his shoulder was clenched tight against his body. The further he advanced on the treacherous log, the more he felt it sag beneath his weight. Reciting his message like a prayer, he advanced steadily and stepped boldly onto the boulder. Under his moccasins, the surface was wet and slippery. It demanded just the right balance and judgment to propel himself off the boulder onto the lower rock some feet further into the foaming creek and then to land that jump with the second jump to the bank already in fluid motion. But Barnabas had absolute faith in his body. It had never failed him, and he willed it not to fail him now. Nor did it. He leaped and then the second jump onto the bank, like two long steps. He was already running as he scrambled up the opposite bank.

The trail angled up the steep slope of the ravine, narrow and muddy from the wet boot heels of earlier runners. His calves began to burn. His breath came shorter. Mud sucked at his moccasins. But the thought of losing to an hourglass spurred him on in his ascent of this cursed hillside.

As he crested the ravine and broke free of the trees, Barnabas dropped off a short bank onto the highway to Green's Crossing, the very spot where he and Ned had first encountered the yellow-haired young man. Now, it was a sprint against the hourglass. On the hard-packed surface, Barnabas notched his speed faster. His moccasins seemed to barely touch the road, and in his mind he recited over and over Sergeant Joshua's curious message.

As the shadows melted into dusk, Barnabas entered the outskirts of Green's Crossing. He passed the tavern where men congregated on the porch and shouted encouragement. Hearing the cheers, Sergeant Joshua and Corporal Sharpe spun on their heels, watching the youth speed toward them. The sergeant looked down at the hourglass, judging how little sand was left. It appeared Barnabas might bowl the burly sergeant over, but he stopped smartly just feet in front of him. Barely panting, he handed the leather pouch over. "Every grain of sand accounted for, Sergeant."

"Well, lad, you made fine time of your run, but can you repeat, word for word, the message I gave you near an hour ago." His hand on the hourglass, he lowered his head and tilted his ear toward Barnabas, who leaned in and whispered the message into it, word for word.

Sergeant Joshua's eyes widened, and he stepped back. "You *are* a runner. And the first to beat the hourglass ever."

TWO

THE CHALLENGE

Military life had become a serious business. The Locke cousins and their new friend, the yellow-haired Georgie Crawley, in company with other recruits, marched west to their posting at Fort Ticonderoga on the New York side of Lake Champlain. The fort had recently passed into the hands of the Continental Army and was under the command of General Arthur St. Clair, who had urgently requested a company of rangers as reinforcements. Whitcomb's Rangers saw their first skirmishes in pursuit of Indian and Loyalist scouting and raiding parties.

The Locke cousins were amazed when they first marched through the gate onto the parade ground of Fort Ticonderoga. They had seen nothing like it. The fort was built of stone barely a generation before by the French, who designed its defenses facing south. Then, the British seized it. The cousins remembered cheering at the news when the fort's undermanned British garrison had been surprised and taken by Ethan Allen's Green Mountain Boys just two springs earlier. How, they wondered, could they defend this vulnerable fort when the enemy would come from the north, and the cannons faced south? Sergeant Joshua pointed out to his recruits that the fort's defenses and those of Mount Independence, on a peninsula jutting northward from the Vermont side, were being hastily strengthened. However, Mount Defiance, a 900-foot elevation looming to the southeast, remained an undefended strategic weakness. The cousins were learning the logistics of warfare.

In discussion with the staff of the fort's quartermaster, the highly efficient Lieutenant Colonel Udney Hay, Sergeant Joshua took a discreet hand in pushing his recruits into key assignments. Recognizing Ned's steadiness and ability to read and cipher, the sergeant recommended Ned be attached as a clerk to the quartermaster's staff. That assignment suited both the sergeant and Ned well. Provisions, scarce clothing, munitions and materiel were ordered, processed, and distributed through the quartermaster's office, like apples picked, packed and delivered. The sergeant took satisfaction in having his own man in this essential hub of activity so that the Rangers would get their fair share. Reconciling himself to two years in the military, Ned hoped for promotion as well as glory.

Georgie Crawley, a cheerful comrade with an easy manner and ready laugh, presented himself as a skilled joiner. Carpenters, workmen and wagoners all reported to the quartermaster's office. Georgie was assigned to a work crew, under the command of the newly promoted Sergeant Sharpe, engaged in necessary repairs throughout the neglected fort and across the narrows in the new fortifications being erected on Mount Independence. When their paths crossed, as they often did when Barnabas delivered messages on foot between the fort and Mount Independence, Georgie liked to pause for tidbits of gossip.

Barnabas had been tested and proven in his role as company courier, much of his time spent covering contested terrain between Captain Whitcomb's company in Fort Ticonderoga and Captain Thomas Lee's company back in New Hampshire, both companies under Captain Whitcomb's command. When his routes accommodated a horse and rider, Barnabas asked expressly for the small bay he had ridden in the race against the hourglass. The little horse was tough, agile and quick. Someone with a musical turn had named him "Presto," but Barnabas called him "Little Bay." He always bore in mind Sergeant Joshua's admonition that it was his duty to deliver the message as it might cost the lives of his fellows should he fail.

Barnabas's speed, reliability and wilderness skills had not gone unnoticed. Having earned

Captain Whitcomb's trust as a courier, Barnabas seemed a likely candidate for special assignments. The captain sought men who could serve as his eyes and ears in the wilderness, reporting to him alone, just as he had served in the preceding war against the French and their allied Indians. A recent deadly incursion into Canada had earned him British enmity and a fat reward for his capture. Perhaps he saw a bit of himself in young Barnabas Locke.

Shortly after reveille one soggy morning in early June, Sergeant Joshua approached Barnabas privately with a message. "Report to Captain Whitcomb in the subalterns' quarters after dark. Make it discreet, lad, and say nothing to anyone." To the sound of a lone fifer practicing the tune Yankee Doodle Dandy and to bursts of laughter and song from open windows, Barnabas strode across the parade ground to the officers' quarters in the dusk of early evening. The rain had slowed to a drizzle. Barnabas had been pondering what this clandestine meeting with the captain could be about, racking his mind for any recent misdemeanor. Before he knocked on the door, a chill that had nothing to do with the weather ran through him—that prickling of senses when a person felt watched. He chided himself, "Of course, I'm being watched. Nearly two thousand men are crowded into this little stone fort. You can't go to the latrine without being watched." But there *was* a singular pair of eyes observing him.

"Enter," he heard and pushed the heavy door open with only the light of oil lamps illuminating the interior. This quarter was reserved for subalterns, the most junior commissioned officers. The upper floors were occupied by senior officers, where no private was permitted. Captain Whitcomb was bent over a long table, reviewing maps with his junior staff. Barnabas snapped to attention. "Private Locke reporting as ordered." The captain turned his attention from the map table. "Gentlemen," he addressed his staff, "may I have a moment with Private Locke."

The junior lieutenants filed out good-naturedly, a few smirking at the private still standing at attention. When the door was closed behind them, the captain said, "At ease. Relax, Private Locke, you're not here for discipline." With his customary directness, he got right to the point. "On the contrary, your performance in the field of action has been more than satisfactory. I require a volunteer with the right skills for an assignment. If you feel you cannot meet this challenge, you may turn around and walk out the door. No consequences will follow you."

Barnabas stared at the captain. Yet without hesitation, he agreed, "I will, Sir."

"But you don't know anything about this mission," the captain stressed. "It will be dangerous. You may not come back."

"Every time I run as a courier, I may not come back, Sir." A note of defiance had crept into Barnabas's voice. He felt he had already proved his courage. Then he softened his tone, "I will be honored, Sir, to accept any assignment you make."

"Very well, Private. Your assignment—here, come look at the map, and I'll show you," and the captain unrolled a map onto the table. With a sweep of his hand, he said, "This is where I want you to go, Private." Barnabas, too, leaned over the table, studying the map laid out before them. He recognized the territory called Coos, the northern reaches of both Vermont and New Hampshire just south of the Canadian border. There, his father had traded with the Abenaki and other tribes, and there, he had spent his youthful years in the company of his father's fur-trapping partners. "I know this region well, Sir. My father took me on trading missions here. I know the terrain, and I know the people, white and Abenaki. And I speak Abenaki. Enough French, too."

"This I knew, Private. I fought with Frederick Locke during the preceding war when we both served as scouts for Rogers' Rangers. Your father was a fine ranger and a man his fellows could trust. I believe you are of the same stamp. I need eyes and ears. I need you to travel in your buckskins, on foot, light and quiet. You know the people of those parts, as you say, white and Indian, and you can speak to them but guard against exposing yourself as a ranger. Out of uniform, such as they are, you run the risk of being taken for a spy." The captain looked sharply into Barnabas's face to gauge his resolve. But Barnabas was scanning the map.

The captain resumed, "I need you to record in your mind, you understand, everything you see and hear, no matter how trifling. Nothing in writing. Pay special attention to the lakeshore, to traffic on the lake, to troop movements, to scouting parties, to anything that hints of secret preparations. And when you've gathered enough to satisfy yourself of its urgency, report back to me posthaste but no later than in a month's time. Think, Private. What questions do you have?"

Barnabas thought. He thought of his cousin Ned. "When do I start, Sir? What provisions do I take? May I say farewell to my cousin first?" He had no fear for himself, but he recognized instinctively the danger.

Captain Whitcomb shook his head. "No, Private, no one is to know or even guess. Sergeant Joshua will give a story if needed. You go tonight at moonrise. The good sergeant is waiting outside this door with your kit." He smiled down at Barnabas' buckled leather shoes. "You can't travel with those on your feet. You'll find your own moccasins and buckskins with Sergeant Joshua. Now, go with God's speed."

Closing the door behind him, Barnabas realized that neither the captain nor Sergeant Joshua had doubted his acceptance of the challenge.

THREE

A GREAT EMBARRASSMENT

Barnabas fell into step with Sergeant Joshua, waiting on the other side of the heavy door. They left the fort by the northern gate, the sergeant saying a quiet word to the sentry. As they followed the path around the fort to the boat landing, a rising full moon lit the waters of Lake Champlain. A lampless boat with an oarsman was waiting to row Barnabas across the narrows to the Vermont shore. The oars were muffled, and the oarsman silent.

Sergeant Joshua gave Barnabas final instructions. "You'll find your blanket roll, clothes and kit wrapped in a bundle. A small sack of cornmeal and pemmican cakes is in there, too. You'll be foraging soon enough. When you return, signal with one shot from this pistol," and the sergeant pressed a fine, German-made pistol into his hands. "A boatman will be stationed nearby to row you back when you make the signal shot." Barnabas tucked the pistol into his belt alongside his trusty tomahawk. It felt heavy.

They shook hands. Barnabas took his seat in the bow, finding the bundle at his feet beneath. As the oarsman and the sergeant pushed the boat into the lapping water, he stripped himself of his uniform and pulled his buckskins from the bundle. They felt warm and smooth against his skin. When the oarsman had reached the midpoint in the narrows, Barnabas, feeling that same odd prickle of being observed, glanced over his shoulder. Just as he did, the full moon cleared clouds, lighting the western bank. On a ledge of rock above the landing, a figure, almost familiar but certainly not the sergeant, stood looking over the narrows. For an instant, the moon revealed a gleam of yellow. Barnabas nearly raised his arm to wave. Then, the figure turned aside toward another taller figure, and the clouds reclaimed the moon and swallowed the two figures in darkness.

When the oarsman beached the boat onto the muddy eastern shore, Barnabas, still in bare feet, leaped over the bow. The oarsman finally spoke. "One month from now, by the moon, I'll be here awaiting your signal shot." Barnabas nodded and gave a strong push on the stern. The boat drifted away silently.

Barnabas scrambled up the bank and ran on bare feet into the wood line. Inside the protection of the trees, he found a likely spot—a cavity within rocks—to stash the bundle of his discarded clothes and shoes. Like the buckskins, his moccasins felt at home on his feet. Turning north along the eastern shore, he ran on under the light of the fitful moon.

Just before daylight, he peered out alertly from underneath his blanket, blessing the sergeant for giving him a woolen one of good weight. Before rising, he listened intently to the morning noises. Gulls and terns were fishing along the shore. Forest birds were awakening. No one on two feet appeared to be nearby. He rose and took stock of what he had at hand. Munching yesterday's pemmican cake, he went meticulously through his kit, making sure he had dry powder, balls and a flint for the pistol. His fire-making tin held a striker, flint and a goodly supply of blackened char cloths to catch the spark. There was a small tin pot for boiling water, as well as a tin of loose tea leaves. His own necessaries kit was intact, and a few other personal items were safely stowed, including his indispensable patch knife to hang around his neck. Satisfied that Sergeant Joshua had sent him on this scouting mission well equipped, he tucked all the gear into its oiled linen haversack. Then he shook out his blanket and tied it into a roll, slinging it over his right shoulder and the haversack over his left. The heavy pistol he tucked into his belt and his tomahawk in its rightful place on his right hip. He turned north, munching another dry cake, and washed it down with a few scoops from the first trickle of fresh water he crossed.

Plunged into this assignment without warning, Barnabas was just now strategizing a plan to accomplish his mission. He could travel the lakeshore quicker, but that course would expose him to both the Abenaki and the Mohawks, for whom the lake was the frontier of their traditional lands. He had close connections with the Abenaki, fewer with the haughty Mohawks, and no clear idea of where their allegiances lay at present. Or, he could go inland, more slowly, through the Green Mountains, following familiar paths north into friendlier, more settled territory. He hoped to communicate with his uncle Edward, Ned's father, on his farm. He kept firmly fixed in his mind that his mission demanded his presence as quick as his feet could take him to the borderlands with Canada. That was where he would center his intelligence gathering. He recognized the risk of capture, both by redcoats and Indians, but that did not deter him.

He decided to go inland, figuring he could travel the distance to the border in four days if he kept a consistent running pace, as was the Indian custom. The sergeant's generous supply of cornmeal and pemmican should last him that long. If he reached his uncle Edward's farm, he could resupply himself there and hear what rumors must be circulating through the region.

He would use the trails traveled by his father for years in his trade with his Indian partners. Barnabas's sense of direction was keenly honed, instinct further sharpened by his father's habit of pointing him to a destination and leaving him to find his way there and home again. He left the shoreline and traveled deeper into the forest on a northeastern course until he crossed one of these trails at midday. He read the growth of the forest around him, the path beneath his moccasins, and holding a licked finger into the air, he found his direction. On an established path, he cautiously made good time, settling into a comfortable, sustainable pace but always aware that someone could be met around the next bend.

Late afternoon of the third day, he scrambled suddenly for cover when he saw through a bend in the trail ahead a glint of metal. He dived behind a screen of mountain laurel and lay low behind a mossy log with the burbling music of a swift-running creek beside him. He prayed that the sound of the creek had muffled his sudden descent into the duff. As a file of Indians swiftly passed, the sun caught the gleam of highly prized metal gorgets worn around their necks and polished silver armbands. They did not look like either Abenaki or Mohawk, but they were wearing warpaint. Barnabas thought they likely were hostiles from one of the Canadian tribes.

Lying there, taking shallow breaths, his eyes caught the glimmer of brook trout flashing through the clear water. Fish! What a welcome gift after all that dry cornmeal. Slowly reaching his right arm to its full extent, he lowered it gently into the icy water, with his fingers and thumb ready to grasp an unwary fish. His young Abenaki friends had taught him this ancient trick. As a fish brushed against his palm, he closed his hand like a steel trap around the trout. The fish fought for his freedom, but Barnabas quickly pulled it out of the water and tucked the thrashing body under his own. Pleased with his success, Barnabas tried again and, to his astonishment, he caught yet another trout. Using his tomahawk like a knife, he quickly gutted and cleaned his catch and wrapped them in moss into his haversack, anticipating a hot meal farther along the path. He buried the entrails in the duff, leaving no scent to alert other passers-by of any sort.

That evening, he scouted for a safe shelter near water and made camp under an overhanging ledge. He laid a few flat stones together, gathered dry kindling, and got out his tin pail and tea for the luxury of a hot meal. His every movement was quiet and considered. The kindling he gathered was hardwood, not smoky pine, and only enough to cook the fish and heat his water. He fried the two trout on a heated flat stone, boiled the water on another and sat back to enjoy his first hot meal since the mess hall he had left three days ago. "Tomorrow," he thought with satisfaction, "I'll be in my own country."

Late the next afternoon, Barnabas paused above a sweeping valley, watered by the Mississquoi River and in the shadows of the Green Mountains, where a small settlement nestled by a falls. He dropped down out of the forest and headed with purpose toward his uncle Edward Locke's farm on the far outskirts. In the woodlot above the farmstead, he reconnoitered his uncle's small clapboard house with its bigger barn attached. On the slope above the farmstead, he noted an empty fenced pasture where dairy cows should be grazing. The young apple orchard, newly productive, was in white bloom. He spied his uncle's sturdy figure, mending fencing near the wagon path that joined the farm to the hard-packed road. He saw no sign of Zeke, the free man of color employed as the hired hand. His aunt Elizabeth was hanging wash on a line. His younger cousins were out of sight. One of the dogs scented him and barked in his direction, but Barnabas saw his uncle reprimand the dog, who obediently went quiet.

Barnabas, nearly out of the woodlot, retreated quickly when he heard the jingle and tramp of men on the move. Around a bend on the road from the west, an officer wearing the insignia of a British first lieutenant sat astride a high-stepping chestnut, leading a squad of six redcoats on foot. His aunt gathered up her washing and hurried into the house. Uncle Edward ordered the dogs to follow her. He hastily threw down his tools and took his stance at the front path. The lieutenant halted his column directly in front of him. Barnabas could see his uncle's angry gestures and then the officer drawing his sword and flourishing it in his uncle's face.

In a surprisingly shrill voice, the lieutenant shouted a command that scattered his six soldiers around the farmstead, pushing in doors with their bayonets fixed. They entered the house, the barn, the woodshed and the springhouse, even the privy like a search party determined to find its quarry. Barnabas feared for his uncle's family and himself.

Abruptly, two of the redcoats triumphantly emerged from the barn with the hired man Zeke, hay caught in his clothes, at the point of their bayonets. Two returned with squawking chickens under their arms. "Damn," Barnabas swore to himself. He was filled with helpless rage, fists drumming against his thighs. With their captives, the insolent redcoats regrouped and tramped westward from the farm. Zeke, his back straight, marched in their midst. Barnabas hunkered down to rest until dusk. His stomach rumbled, and the released dogs barked again. He saw his uncle gaze upward into the woodlot where he was hiding. The man missed nothing.

As darkness drew in, Barnabas saw the flickering light of a candle in a back window. And when Barnabas knocked gently at that window, Uncle Edward asked in a hopeful voice, "Is Ned with you, Barnabas?" "No, Uncle, it's only me," he replied softly. The bolts slid open on the narrow kitchen door, and Barnabas stepped in. His uncle carried the candle to the table.

His aunt Elizabeth hugged him close. "Tell me, how is my son? Why is Ned not with you?" Barnabas was quick to allay her fears. "He's well, Aunt. Ned's in a safe place and doing important work. I left him thriving, but I cannot say more." He turned to his uncle, but Aunt Elizabeth was already pushing him into a chair at the table where plates of food and tankards of cider were laid ready. He was sorry to disappoint his own family but glad that it was he sitting down before this welcome feast.

His uncle could barely wait until Barnabas had wiped the cloth napkin across his mouth. But Barnabas was even more impatient. "What is happening here? Why did they take Zeke? Where are Sally and little Enoch? Where are the cows?" Questions spilled out of him, and his uncle answered them in turn.

"Zeke has been taken like other able-bodied men to work at the boatyards at St. Johns. The children we have sent to your Aunt Liza's family.

God rot their souls; just yesterday morn, those lobster backs stole most of my cows to put milk in their officers' tea. But Zeke, God bless his quick wits, saved Bess and Joan and tucked them into the little meadow out of sight. I must go soon to milk the poor dears. That thieving lieutenant brought a wagon. They not only drove away the cows, they seized the last of the cider barrels. They'd have seized Zeke, too, but he was too quick for them. But today, Lieutenant Pendleton returned for another purpose. That bloody lieutenant asked for you by name. He was looking for *you*, Barnabas."

His aunt Elizabeth murmured with regret, "But they got poor Zeke anyways."

Startled, Barnabas flung back in his chair. "But how did they know my name? How is it they came to *you* to find me? Why are they looking for me?" He looked at his uncle with a face gone wild. The answer he received was not to his liking. "That fop of a lieutenant accused *you* of being a spy. If they catch you, Barny, they will hang you. That bloody man laughed in my face. He threatened to cut down my orchard if I hid you." He paused for an instant as the thought struck him. "I knew someone was up in the woodlot. Stringer had your scent and whined like a child when I'd not let him go to you."

Under cover of darkness, Barnabas left his uncle's house—his aunt's blessing for him and a

32

message for Ned in his heart, his uncle's warning for caution in his ears, and, for his stomach, fresh provisions wrapped in a cloth and stowed by his aunt in his haversack. Barnabas felt the weight of their trust and vowed to his aunt he would deliver her message word for word to Ned.

He followed the road westward, running by the light of the stars. He nursed a hope that he would eventually come up on the heels of the marching soldiers—and Zeke. If he came upon them, they would be already encamped, perhaps asleep. He would devise some way to rescue Zeke.

In the darkest hours of the night, Barnabas caught the scent of smoke mixed with the savor of roasted chicken. He paused along the roadside to catch its direction. Proceeding with his uncle's caution, he approached warily and was rewarded by the flicker of dying fires and the sleepy stamp of a horse's hoof. Soldiers were encamped in a roadside clearing. Barnabas melted into the woods, silent as a ghost. But there were other ghosts in these woods. Within moments, he was surrounded by tall, dark, silent figures. He knew at once they were Indians.

Barnabas was seized, a hand clamped over his mouth. Two of the figures lifted him off his feet. He thrashed in protest. A quiet voice breathed into his ear, "Barnabas Locke, I am one you know. Be still, and we will talk." Barnabas's heart leaped up in relief. It was someone speaking in the Abenaki language, someone who knew him by name and recognized him in the darkness. He nodded and was deposited on his feet. As one with the Indian party, he faded deeper into the forest.

At a safe distance from the British camp, they talked to one another. "So, it is you, Squando, my good friend." Squando was only a few years older but had undertaken the Abenaki education of Barnabas Locke. He had been a thorough, if impatient, instructor. Barnabas had been a ready pupil. "You still do not see well at night!" Squando chafed him. They clasped arms and laughed together. Barnabas fell easily into Abenaki, the second language of his youth.

"I saw you coming in my dreams last night," Squando informed him in his superior way.

"And what did you see?" Barnabas inquired.

"You were in danger. I was not surprised. But let us return to the matter at hand. I want that bright horse. My friends here want those guns. As to the sword, that will be a gift for our elders to decide."

Barnabas made his claim, "And I want to free the captive man."

With all of them agreeing on those terms, Barnabas then asked, "Do you intend to kill these soldiers?"

"No, that would be an open act of war against the British. My people have not yet decided to ally ourselves with them. They have not honored treaties with us in the past. We liked our French allies better. We admire courage and honor. I think our councils will decide soon. Now, my dreams tell me that this little group of redcoats snoring by their fires will waken to a great embarrassment." He laughed.

As the raiders silently approached the British encampment lit dimly by the embers of dying campfires, they found the posted sentry asleep, having failed first to refresh the fires. He was dispatched with a single blow from a war club. Each Abenaki had marked his own target. While Squando calmed the chestnut with quiet words in its twitching ear, his comrades liberated both guns and boots from the heavily sleeping redcoats. To Barnabas, they seemed almost like sleeping children, innocent in their blankets. But Zeke, he saw with relief, was wide awake, seated against a tree trunk, tightly bound, and watching him. He knelt beside Zeke and, in a bare breath of whisper, said, "Yes, it is Barny, Zeke, come with friends." The black man nodded. With his sharply honed tomahawk, it took only an instant for Barnabas to slice Zeke free of his bonds.

Barnabas chuckled to himself as the raiding party returned jubilantly to the designated rendezvous. "Bootless, unarmed and horseless," he thought, "a great embarrassment in truth."

Squatting together with Squando and Zeke, Barnabas made a further request of his Abenaki friend. "Will you give sanctuary to my friend Zeke here within your village? Only until such time as he deems it safe to return to my uncle's employment or wherever he chooses to go. Zeke is a man of 'courage and honor.'" Squando smiled to hear his own words repeated to him and placed his hand on Zeke's arm. "You will be as my black brother, Zeke."

Mindful of his mission, Barnabas seized this moment of camaraderie to question them both. "Tell me what you believe to be happening among the British and those tribes allied with them? Why are they stealing men and provisions?" Zeke promptly replied, "The redcoats are building gunboats and barges at the new shipyard at St. Johns. Those lobster backs had loose tongues. They boasted about rewards for each working man they deliver. And, Barny, there's a big one on *your* head."

Squando offered his observations. "There is much debate amongst the councils of our elders. They are weighing the opinions of our chiefs and the wisdom of our peacemakers. We Abenaki have not yet announced for war, but our foes, the Haudenosaunee, the Iroquois as you call that confederation, have split in their alliances, as might we. The Tuscarora and the Oneida will back their trading partners among the colonists, but the others

36

are allying with the redcoats. All of us must protect our trade. Also, we must defend our lands from you colonists. Already, the warriors of Canada are on the move southward as allies with the British. They are raiding the border settlements and those places to the west of the great lake you call Champlain. We have seen them boldly trespassing across our own lands. This much, at least, you can be sure is true. Whatever my visions show me, Barny, I will never be at war with you."

Barnabas sat back on his heels, thinking hard. He wondered how much of what Squando had confided would hold until he met with Captain Whitcomb. He must find a safe place to watch for the fleet now being assembled upriver at St. Johns. That would place him at the Canadian border, where the Richelieu River flowed into a narrow neck of the lake. Risky but necessary. He needed to know the moment the British troops, and how many, arrived at Lake Champlain. He would count hard, memorizing every gunboat and its guns, estimating provisions, and calculating the number of soldiers on each vessel. Then, it would be a race between himself and the water-borne fleet the 120 miles to Fort Ticonderoga. He needed to cross the lake, and he knew the man who could make that passage happen.

Squando, leading his bright horse, and his comrades loaded with booty departed into the night. Barnabas and Zeke made a hearty farewell before Zeke departed after them. Everyone seemed well pleased with their good fortune. Barnabas spared a last thought for the arrogant Lieutenant Pendleton, who was now walking barefoot toward a certain court-martial and a sentry who was walking with a very sore head.

FOUR

THE HOUNDS

In fading light on the following day, Barnabas stood with a wiry man on the small, empty landing where the Mississquoi Bay emptied into Lake Champlain. Across the narrows stretched the broad, marshy tongue of land, claimed by Vermont, that pushed down from the Canadian border into the lake. On its far side, close to the border, Barnabas planned to observe any movement south onto the lake. He had hoped the old man would ferry him across this narrow passage of rough water, but there was no ferry boat docked at the landing.

"I am not surprised to see you, young Barnabas Locke," said the wiry man in heavily accented English. "Your name is being spoken in these parts. Alas, in British mouths. A reward is attached to your head, *mon ami*. But perhaps this you already know?" The Frenchman had been a trusted colleague of the senior Mr. Locke. His missus, a round, smiling Abenaki woman, had often welcomed

Barnabas into their home. She had already tapped his belly, eager to put food into it.

"I have business on the western side, Jean-Pierre, and you have put your finger on my need of discretion. Yet I see no boat here." Barnabas looked about with an uneasy feeling.

Jean-Pierre Bellevue spat a stream of scurrilous words. "The wicked redcoats have burned my darling Marguerite. What harm could a small boat do them? But," and the Frenchman patted Barnabas's arm, "Do not fear, *mon jeune ami*. I have a canoe, hidden in the marsh grass, old but still trustworthy. You will paddle yourself across. Hide it well off the track. British gunboats are patrolling these waters, searching every craft. They are insolent in their trespass." And he spat into the water lapping at his feet. "I think perhaps there is no more business for Jean-Pierre in these parts."

With no time to waste and with good food in his stomach and another packet of fresh provisions in his haversack, Barnabas launched the birchbark canoe into the rough waters of the narrows. It was a strenuous paddle under the light of a waning moon, but he thought himself unseen. On the opposite shore of marshy pine lands, he found a safe spot under a broken tree to wedge the canoe and covered it with debris. He easily found the cart track Jean-Pierre had indicated and set off through the pine lands for the opposite shore.

In the following days of June, Barnabas watched intently for movement south onto the lake, for movement by troops, Indians, and mercenary Hessians, and for the passage and increasing frequency of patrolling gunboats. He moved his simple camp every few days to avoid becoming complacent. The cover was thick, but there was no high ground to observe at a safe distance. When he wasn't watching, he was foraging—berries and mushrooms, birds' eggs, crabs, and crawdads became staples of his diet. By night, he trapped fish within the inlets of the marsh. Black flies were swarming and a constant irritant. He daubed every part of exposed skin with mud or the charcoal remains of his tiny fires. He found a sort of comfort in watching the fires at Rouses Point across the thin finger of lake between the marshland and New York. Other campfires dotted the shoreline north as far as he could see. Often, the sound of hammering late into the night and bursts of laughter or cursing bounced off the lake water, exciting his curiosity.

Barnabas was driven to explore ever farther northward into Canadian territory. He chose the fringes of light at dawn and dusk when he could blend seamlessly into the landscape. He discovered, moored in coves and inlets along the coast, many new small craft and some surprisingly large two-decker gunboats already moved downstream from the boatyards. He knew little of boat building but did know that new wooden craft needed "taking up," meaning the green lumber must swell and shrink until it no longer took on water, particularly under the weight of troops and munitions. Workmen, sweating in the June heat in shirtsleeves, were busy applying tar, fitting vessels with oars and oarlocks, masts and rigging, decks, and painting ship names on bows. He would remember "Thunderer," an enormous double-decker with oddly slanted gunwales. But of most interest to Barnabas was the number of vessels with swivel cannons mounted on their bows and the multiple cannons on the two-decker galleys. The increasing numbers made his brain feverish.

However, his father had taught him an ingenious method of counting. He had kept track of the number of pelts traded with each partner by tying knots into a length of colored yarn. Each color of yarn signified the trading partner and his pelts. Each knot signified a count of ten. When Barnabas had spied his aunt Elizabeth's basket of stocking yarn, he had thought to ask her for a sufficient number of lengths in different colors. Now, he devised a private scheme for tracking the type and number of craft, the number and poundage of cannons, and the number and kind of troops— redcoat, Indian, Hessians, who he learned wore the insignia of artillerists. Each day, the number of knots grew alarmingly.

He slept fitfully, mostly through the hot middle hours of the day, swatting mosquitoes in his sleep. Sometimes, after he had returned from his evening scouting, he fell into a deeper sleep when he dreamed of a half-familiar figure outlined against a darkening sky, a face almost sharpening into focus. Day and night, his stomach rumbled. His moccasins wore thin. He knew he was pressing himself too hard.

On one evening foray, eavesdropping on drunken conversation around a campfire, Barnabas overheard several redcoats speculating when they would begin boarding. It seemed they had received orders for deployment and were lambasting "Gentleman Johnny" Burgoyne for landing them in this fly-invested swamp. Barnabas took special note of that general's name. When one inebriated redcoat unexpectedly rose to relieve his bladder, he blundered toward the very tree that Barnabas was sheltering behind. Barnabas's right hand tightened around his tomahawk. The noise of urine splattering against the tree and the soldier's grunts of relief muffled his careful backward retreat.

He laughed to himself after that misadventure. But only days later, he faced the most dangerous threat thus far. In his piney shelter under the hot sun, Barnabas was calculating the passage of days. A shadow passing his face alerted him to buzzards circling overhead. "Do I stink like carrion?" he wondered. He flapped his hands upwards to alert the buzzards that he was not their next meal. The buzzards caught an updraft and soared away. But other eyes had been watching the buzzards circle. Three Huron materialized within spitting distance, and Barnabas went as still as a fawn in his tangle of fallen pines.

The Huron were stripped to loincloths and leggings, their bronze upper torsos tattooed, and their painted faces intently scouring the ground for signs. He felt sure the Indians could smell the fear soaking him. Like the buzzards, they were hunting prey, and that prey was likely him. Had he left careless signs in soft ground? Had his canoe been discovered? Had his faint outline been seen in the night? Was he somehow arousing the hunting instincts innate in native warriors? He held his breath until they finally passed on.

Trembling, he fought against his impulse to stay just one day longer, to gather just one more important fact, to overhear just one more telling conversation—an impulse he recognized to be dangerous not only to his own life but to that of his mission. He heard voices in his head. Captain Whitcomb's instruction to return "as quick as you can the moment you know you have enough." His aunt Elizabeth's loving message to her son and the hoarse voice of Sergeant Joshua's warning that "failure to deliver your message might cost the lives of your fellows."

Knowing that the Huron would not halt in their search, he waited until the moon rose, readying himself for departure. He braided the lengths of knotted yarn like a belt around his narrow waist beneath his hunting shirt. He padded the contents of his haversack so that nothing jingled—another trick his father had taught him. He slung bedroll and haversack over his shoulders, searched the ground beneath his feet for any loose part of kit, and climbed out of the shelter of the deadfall. He turned his face southeast, finding again the cart track that led to his borrowed canoe. God willing, it was safe where he had hidden it.

Under the uncertain moon, obscured by scudding clouds, Barnabas picked his way with great but urgent caution, his ears nearly swiveling on his head, his eyes alert for any outline, any movement. He spared a thought for Squando. "I'll never let him say again that I can't see at night." He knew his tracks would be evident to keen Huron eyes and that his pursuers would pick up his trail at daylight. He hoped to have retrieved the canoe and crossed the narrows by dawn. He had just enough hours to make that distance to the safe harbor of Jean-Pierre Bellevue's trading post.

Then, to his horror, he spied the faint flicker of torches behind. Those damnable Huron were following his sign by the light of torches. It now was a footrace. He abandoned caution, his feet flying. Occasionally, he cast an eye over his shoulder, watching the torchlight gain in brightness. The Hurons were seasoned runners, and, in his depleted state, he knew he could not outrun them, and yet, each time, he ran a little faster. Like a laughing fool, he giggled, "The hounds of Hell *are* on my heels!"

The pine growth thinned, and he thankfully glimpsed moonlight reflecting off the water. From deep within himself, he summoned another burst of speed. In his head, he envisioned just where he had buried the canoe under debris at the foot of a snapped-off pine. The snag of the broken trunk stood like a sentinel, and he raced toward it unerringly. He dug the canoe forth and carried it across the shore. He had no sooner balanced himself on his knees and dug deep with his first strokes of the paddle when his pursuers erupted onto the stony shore. Furious at the sight of their quarry already pulling away, two of the three plunged to their waists into the water, struggling to catch the canoe with grasping hands. The taller grabbed the gunwale, violently shaking the canoe, trying to capsize Barnabas. Before the second warrior could grab the other side, Barnabas whipped the tomahawk from his belt. He arched his body backward, slashing the blade downward across the fingers of the first warrior, cleaving two fingers from that hand. The warrior screamed and grasped his mutilated hand with the other. The face of the second warrior, black and red with paint, rose out of the water at Barnabas's left shoulder. He instinctively swung the heavy paddle edgewise like an ax, cracking the man across his brow and nose. The Huron sank back into the water. Digging the paddle deep, Barnabas propelled the canoe forward.

When breath returned to his body, the canoe was in the middle of the narrow passage, carried by the current to the eastern shore but north of Jean-Pierre's trading post. Barnabas was too exhausted to correct course but used the paddle to steer the canoe in the right direction. Silently gliding into reeds some distance above the landing, Barnabas stowed the canoe safely. He took up his gear and started toward the trading post as the sun cleared the trees to the east. Skirting a little cove, he saw the glint of sunlight on metal below him and recognized with shock a gunboat moored to a stout stump along the bank. A four-pounder was mounted on the bow. "Blast!" Barny cursed under his breath. "They're back. Looks like a surprise attack, the bastards."

From Jean-Pierre's trading post rose angry voices. Barnabas heard one uncannily familiar voice, shrilling commands. A plan, a desperate one, sprang into Barnabas's mind and then into action. If he were to save his friends, he must create a diversion. The gunboat presented itself as a candidate. Swiftly, he removed all the oars but one that he left dangling into the water. The rest he heaved into the reeds and sawgrass. Then, scooping up mud, he packed the barrel of the swivel cannon mounted on the bow. With one slash of his tomahawk, the boat was unmoored. Now, he pushed it outward and into the current. He prayed it would float temptingly past the landing.

He moved landward, using the woods behind the trading post to shield his approach. Ducking behind a woodshed, he pulled the pistol from his belt and poured dry powder into the flashpan. As he peeked around the front corner of the shed, he pulled the pistol to half-cock. Standing in front of the trading post, five Hessians in green coats and a British Second Lieutenant menaced Jean-Pierre and his missus at rifle point, roundly abusing them with blows and threats. Barnabas was outgunned but determined to put the soldiers to a rout. From his vantage, he saw the gunboat floating idly by as though on a pleasure outing. The angry voices suddenly erupted into German shouts and one high-pitched English voice, commanding the Hessians to "Stop it! Stop it!" Barnabas grinned.

He watched as three of the Hessians darted down to the shore, stripped themselves to their shirts and plunged into the water. Their boots, clothes and arms lay in tempting piles on the shore. Barnabas eyed the Hessians' Jaeger rifles with interest. The Hessians floundered to the boat, all three of them clumsily trying to board on the same side. When they nearly upended the vessel, one of them swam to the other side as a counterweight, and all three pulled themselves aboard by the gunwales. The lieutenant—a second lieutenant—screamed instructions and scorn on his Hessians, brandishing a short sword in the air as he hopped in rage near the water's edge. Left behind as guards, two Hessians had turned their attention from Jean-Pierre and his missus, watching the farcical rescue of their gunboat and smiling grimly behind their lieutenant's back.

Barnabas seized the moment. As did Jean-Pierre, who flung himself against the broad green back of the Hessian who stood closest, knocking him to the ground and pummeling him while his quick-witted missus pulled away the Hessian's Jaeger. As the second Hessian spun about and lifted his rifle and aimed, he was suddenly deterred by the cold impress of a pistol to his temple. And by the sound of a hammer clicking to full cock. Gingerly, he lowered the gun which Missus Bellevue snatched away.

On the hapless gunboat, the three Hessians were shouting German oaths and pointing urgently, not to their comrade with a pistol at his head or to the Hessian being manhandled by the Bellevues, but to a greater danger emerging from the forest. One mercenary seized the swivel gun and aimed it at the small band of Abenakis, one tall, familiar figure leading an excited horse, now crossing the clearing. With a striker, the Hessian triggered the mud-packed four-pounder, which promptly exploded in a red flash and a cloud of gray smoke. The Hessian was blown into the water, and the shock of concussion knocked the other two off their feet.

Squando, dropping the reins and whooping an Abenaki war cry, sprinted ahead of his band into the melee, swinging his war club. At last, the lieutenant at the landing spun around and discovered his entire detachment rendered out of action. Belatedly, he raised his pistol, but the gun misfired. The lieutenant had no opportunity to reprime the pistol as two warriors seized him and dragged him to the feet of Squando. Other warriors scooped up the prized rifles littering the shore and aimed them at the Hessians, now wobbling to their feet on the disabled gunboat. The Hessians mustered the effort to retrieve their nearly drowned fellow before stroking awkwardly with the lone oar back to shore. Met by jubilant Abenakis, they were herded up the bank to join their subdued lieutenant and fallen comrades. Other Abenaki scavenged their discarded boots and clothing, trying them on and fingering the fancy brass buttons.

Barnabas and Squando briefly embraced. Both friends were made happy, for differing reasons, when Zeke joined them, leading the fractious chestnut from the woods by its Indian war bridle. From the clump of prisoners huddled together in their skivvies, the Second Lieutenant shrilled, "That's my horse!"

The name finally came to Barnabas, who addressed the blustering officer guilelessly, "It appears you have lost a star from your shoulder, Second Lieutenant Pendleton. A pity that I must inform you that your horse has been requisitioned by the Continental Army." Perhaps the full enormity of this second disastrous encounter with Barnabas Locke and his Abenaki allies began to penetrate the lieutenant's British armor. His protests rang hollow.

Missus Bellevue emerged from her cabin door, shouldering a woven reed basket laden with provisions. Jean-Pierre soon reappeared at the landing, paddling his recovered canoe into which he had tossed one of the gunboat's oars. He went into the woodshed to retrieve his rifle and other necessaries where he had hidden them in the expectation that the British would return. The Bellevues had only awaited Barnabas's return of their canoe and worked in wordless tandem to execute their plan for a speedy departure.

Barnabas and Squando assessed the situation. Too many parties held a stake in this morning's outcome. They hit upon the simplest solution to dispose of the gunboat raiders—sending them back, sans weapons, clothing, boots, and honor in the damaged gunboat, provided only with a single pair of oars. Lieutenant Pendleton was forced, politely, to surrender his short sword and pistol. He was permitted to keep his clothes but not his boots.

"Reparation for the burning of Marguerite," Barnabas said as he relieved the fuming lieutenant of the silver coins found in his waistcoat pocket. He presented them with a flourish to Jean-Pierre.

"You sorry thief, you'll swing for this," Pendleton threatened through gritted teeth, but Barnabas only laughed into the blazing blue eyes. The sorry lot of injured and dazed Hessians were bundled aboard as the Abenakis jeered and flourished their newly acquired rifles above their heads. Barnabas doubted the shrill lieutenant would be given yet a third command by his superiors.

The Bellevues announced they were paddling down the lake on the first leg of their venture into the Ohio Country. "Wars are not good for business," Jean-Pierre had long opined, and he was itching for new trading opportunities. He and his wife said their adieus, the kind missus pressing a small deerskin bag of dried pemmican into Barnabas's hands. With grateful thanks, he tied the bag to his belt.

Barnabas promptly traded the lieutenant's sword and pistol, as well as the lieutenant's shot and powder bag, to Squando in exchange for the British horse, also once the lieutenant's property. Squando was certain he had the better of the bargain. "British horses are more trouble than they are worth. Made for parade grounds, not for forest trails." Barnabas privately thought his friend was right. Eyeing the horse, who was tossing his defiant head and pawing the ground in disdain, Barnabas took the reins of the war bridle from Zeke's hand. He reached up and seized a stiff ear, whispering a warning. "Behave yourself, or I will give you back to the Abenakis, who will feast on you." As the chestnut mulled this over, Barnabas swiftly mounted his bare back.

Calling Zeke to his side, Barnabas unslung his blanket roll and then his haversack, keeping only his kit, and dropped them into Zeke's hands. "Nothing must hinder me on my journey south, but these may help you as you decide your future."

"God's blessings, Barny," and Zeke slapped the side-stepping chestnut on his rump. He watched as Barnabas and the British horse disappeared at a canter on the forest track south.

FIVE

THE SPY

The British horse insisted on his own pace. He would walk, he would trot, he would canter if pressed. He would not run. He was suspicious to his bone. He objected to every untoward object—a sinister, overhanging branch, a stump looming at the side of the road, a sudden drumbeat of grouse, or a squirrel skittering across his path. Intending not so much a name as an insult, Barnabas dubbed him "Macaroni." He was a tall horse with four white stockings and a blazed face, no doubt chosen for his pretty looks by Lieutenant Pendleton when he bought his army commission. Barnabas thought the demoted lieutenant was very like his horse—purely macaroni.

The British Army, like most armies, moved at a snail's pace where Macaroni was most at home. And yet, with his moccasins worn through, his stomach hollow, and his stamina stretched to the snapping point, Barnabas had no choice but to press Macaroni into a reluctant canter. The gait was steady and, to give the horse his due, would have been a comfortable ride had Barnabas a saddle to sit in and stirrups to support his tired legs. He thought with longing for the dependable and responsive Little Bay. These thoughts brought him back to his duties as a scout. But both he and the horse were flagging. Since leaving the trading post two days ago, he had led Macaroni into forest meadows to graze. As the horse cropped grass, Barnabas had leaned against his shoulder, dozing upright with the reins in his hand.

Now, early on this third morning, exhausted and back sore, Barnabas leaned into the horse's neck, dozing. Macaroni slowed to a walk and, finding no resistance from his passenger, proceeded forward on his own recognizance. Then the horse abruptly stopped, jerking Barnabas awake and out of a recurring dream—that half-familiar figure with the glint of gold on the rock. Macaroni stood at full alert, his ears pointing forward, his nostrils flaring, his body quivering. The horse stared at the figure of a man on the road, too distant to distinguish as either friend or foe. Barnabas nudged Macaroni forward, and he reluctantly complied. Slowly, the horse and rider closed the distance. The man on the road did not move. The morning sun sent fingers of light through the green growth and formed a halo of gold around his head. Barnabas urged the horse a few reluctant steps closer. The man on the rock, the man on the road, and the man in the dream fused into one. It was Georgie Crawley.

"It's you, Georgie!" Barnabas shouted in disbelief. A sense of urgent wrongness flooded through him.

"I've been sent to find you, Barny," Georgie called back, "Sergeant Joshua sent me to scout ahead for you. He fears you had been taken by the British or killed." Georgie was babbling nonsense. He looked like a man on the run, fleeing for his own life. As Georgie approached, Barnabas commanded, "Halt there! It was you, Georgie, who stood on the rock watching me being rowed to the Vermont shore. It was you who sent my name and mission ahead of me." Pieces of the puzzle were falling into place. Barnabas felt a palpable danger from this man he had called friend. And Macaroni sensed not only his rider's deep unease but the desperation of the man approaching.

As Georgie suddenly lunged forward, reaching up a hand to grasp the war bridle, Macaroni reared up in outrage. Barnabas tumbled backward over the horse's rump, landing on his feet with his tomahawk already in his hand. Georgie was not so nimble. A flailing front hoof grazed his forehead, knocking him senseless to the ground. Macaroni bolted. He saw his chance to abandon duty and was gone with no more farewell than a flick of his tail and a backward kick.

Barnabas watched the horse go with a shrug of his shoulders. "So you *can* run. Go find your British masters if you like." He turned to the prone figure in the dust. Georgie's head was red with blood, but he was breathing. He kicked his side, and Georgie groaned. Barnabas tugged off the haversack from Georgie's shoulder and quickly searched it for food. He found none, signaling that Georgie had left the fort in a hurry. He did find something of greater interest—the latest of the bound ledgers from the quartermaster's office. Barnabas hurriedly flicked through its detailed lists of munitions, food stocks, and armaments entered in his cousin's careful script. A heavy sheet of official paper fell into his hand. It was a letter from General Gates's headquarters in Albany, notifying General St. Clair at Fort Ticonderoga that reinforcements could not be spared at this time. Barnabas whistled. He tucked the damning evidence back into Georgie's haversack and slung it over his shoulder.

He rolled Georgie over onto his stomach. Finding that the corded reins of the war bridle ripped from Macaroni's jaw were still wrapped in Georgie's hand, Barnabas used one rein to bind his hands together behind his back, adding one more hitch than strictly necessary. The other rein he attached as a leash. He stood over the inert body, panting slightly and yanked on the cord. "Get up," he snarled and yanked again for emphasis.

Georgie crawled painfully to his feet, dazed and bloody. "Please don't kill me, Barny," he pleaded. 'I'm a prisoner of war. I'm your friend."

"You are a spy! You are a traitor! You are not my friend, and nobody knows you are a prisoner of war," Barnabas spat. Pulling his pistol from his belt, he notched it to half-cock. But Georgie had spunk left in him.

"You won't shoot me," he defied Barnabas. "You don't have the gumption for that."

Barnabas drew a deep breath to calm himself. "You're right. I won't deny the hangman." But he left his pistol at half-cock. "Now march! And shut your yap, you lying traitor!"

He pushed Georgie several steps ahead of him to the length of the leash. They shuffled forward, Georgie still dazed from Macaroni's blow. Barnabas was at the end of his rope. He had lost his horse and was now saddled with a prisoner. On this first night of the full moon, he desperately wanted to meet the boatman at their agreed rendezvous. Despite Georgie's litany of complaints—that his hands hurt, that his head hurt, that he was thirsty, that he was hungry, that it was too hot, that he needed to rest—Barnabas remained unmoved. He had his own complaints to suffer. He forced the pace despite stumbling several times over nothing more than a stone or a rut. Lack of sleep and the rigors of the past weeks had taken a physical toll on his young body. He was keenly aware that Georgie would seize any opportunity to turn the tables.

As the weary, dusty hours passed in this uneasy lockstep, Georgie changed his strategy. He sought to goad his captor. He chose to boast rather than to confess. Unmistakably, he was proud of his exploits at Fort Ticonderoga and of his loyalty to his English King George the Third. He boasted to Barnabas about his propertied and prosperous family in Massachusetts and recounted the many ways they had been hounded for that loyalty and that hard-won prosperity. He bragged of his cleverness. He had tried for the position of company runner for a reason—for that ready access to invaluable information. "But no, Barnabas Locke, you took that away from me. Everyone sings your praises while I'm fixing the roofs over their heads." His resentment ran deep. How easy it had been to weasel his way into Ned's confidence, into Sergeant Sharpe's good graces, and into offices and defenses both at Fort Ticonderoga and at the gun batteries on the heights of Mount Independence. With his carpenter's bag and useful tools, he was either welcomed or ignored everywhere. He had found ways to be invisible and yet present when good intelligence was for the picking. He joked and gossiped, and people liked him.

Eventually, his braggadocio outran his discretion. "But your cousin Ned almost ruined everything. He noticed my interest in his work. Yes, I asked questions, perhaps too many. He asked how could I be so busy elsewhere and yet always underfoot." As he aired his grievances, Georgie grew increasingly incautious. "I think he went to Sergeant Sharpe with his suspicions. He had no proof to show, and I was too smart to give him any, but I was running out of time. He turned up like a bad penny when the quartermaster's office should have been empty. He interfered, and for his troubles, I smashed him with a hammer. I think I left him dead!" Georgie caught himself short. "Well, perhaps not dead."

Barnabas yanked him hard. "Turn around." Barnabas brought up the pistol and put it on full cock. If his promise to Ned's mother must be broken, at least she would be avenged.

Georgie faced him squarely, dried blood on his pale face. "Has it occurred to you, Barnabas Locke, that I, too, am a patriot to my cause? We are both Englishmen with the rights and duties of Englishmen. But I hold true to my loyalty to my king and country, and you do not. Yet why must I be the one who hangs? Why not you, Barnabas Locke, you who are the true traitor?"

Barnabas was taken aback by this assault on reason. Yet, he privately acknowledged there might be a kernel of truth in what Georgie said. He rallied his defenses. "But we were never equal as Englishmen. We colonists had no representation. And when we demanded it, as the right of Englishmen, your king sent troops against us, forced us to house them and feed them and then shot us in the streets when we protested. What loyalty did he show to us?"

In reply, Georgie employed a new tactic. "My hands are numb. I can no longer feel them. I'll not take another step forward. Loosen my bonds, or kill me now. The choice is yours."

Barnabas went still in thought. He returned his pistol to his belt at half-cock. "Then turn around," he snapped and stepped close enough to examine Georgie's hands. They had turned white. They looked strangled. He weighed the risks. To loosen the knots would require his own two hands. Even injured, Georgie was just that much stronger than he that he might well turn on him. And yet Barnabas could scarcely march the man forward if he refused to move. He barked, "Down on your face."

Georgie immediately sank to his knees and squirmed onto his stomach. His captor straddled his legs, pinning Georgie into the dust. He felt Barnabas struggle with the knots on his wrists. He prepared himself for the moment the bonds loosened, and when they did, with all his remaining strength, Georgie wrenched his hands free,

61

humped up and rolled to the side, dislodging Barnabas from his back. With one freed hand, he yanked the half-cocked pistol from Barnabas's belt. Staggering, he got to his feet. Barnabas had instinctively grabbed for his 'hawk, but was an eye blink too late. Suddenly, it was he facing the barrel of a fully cocked pistol. The face of the man holding it was intractable.

"Take off my haversack. Throw it at my feet." Georgie's voice was cold and ruthless. He had prevailed and had no pity in him. "Unlike you, Barnabas Locke, I can pull this trigger."

A sound, like the swooshing of a peregrine falcon, was followed by a solid thud. Georgie's startled eyes went large. The point of an arrow protruded through his chest. He looked down at it in disbelief. His face went bloodless, but his final words were clear, "Tell my father I was loyal to my oath." Then his eyes emptied, and he fell lifeless.

Squando emerged like an apparition from the forest. "Again, I have saved your life, my friend Barny," Squando greeted him. "I had a dream about you and have followed you for a day and a night. And then that useless British horse passed at full gallop like a messenger from you. Is there food in that haversack?"

"No food," Barnabas said, shouldering the haversack, "but proof that this man was a spy." He fingered the knotted cords beneath his shirt.

"When the moon is high, I must be at the narrows of the lake. I am feeling a little spent, Squando. Will you accompany me in the event I falter?" He wearily bent to retrieve the pistol that had fallen into the dust.

The two friends carried the dead man off the track and left him under a pine, buried in the thick fall of needles, the site marked by a large flat rock leaning against the tree like a headstone. Barnabas looked down without regret at the man who could have been himself.

SIX

THE PISTOL

Thunder rumbled, and black clouds thickened. A westerly wind rose and whistled through the swaying trees. Squando squinted into the darkening sky. "I think we will not outrun this storm. You limp with weariness, and I, too, am tired.

Barnabas had spent the past weeks living rough—besieged by swarms of black flies, mosquitoes, and sudden summer storms. He would not seek shelter when he had come this close to his destination. Now, his worries were compounded by fear for Ned. It was painful to imagine him dead and that this must be the message he would deliver to Aunt Elizabeth and Uncle Edward. He and his friend talked as they hastened onward.

"Squando, tonight a boatman will come to the sound of my pistol shot to row me across the narrows. I can have no rest until my mission is accomplished." Again, he touched the cords at his waist through his shirt.

Squando nodded in agreement. "And I must sleep through a night without dreams of you in danger." Squando raised a hand to signify a more serious matter. "Word among my people is this. If the English take Fort Ticonderoga and then Albany, retribution would be fierce against us if we allied with the colonists. If the French end their silence and declare for your patriots, then we will do so, too. We hope the colonists will treat with us as honorably as have the French, but this remains debated among our elders. Much depends on the success of this General Burgoyne, who even now sails to your Fort Ticonderoga. A great fleet of gunboats and barges packed with soldiers and cannon spilled into the lake like spawning salmon two days after we parted at Bellevue ferry."

Barnabas weighed the import of his words carefully. "Then you will not be crossing the narrows with me?" Squando nodded. Barnabas understood that, although his friend had rescued him, he had come in pursuit of Barnabas to carry a message directly from the councils of his people—to impart this final confirmation that the British fleet had sailed and that the Abenakis awaited the outcome of the battle to come. But, out of friendship, Squando would see him to safety.

"Now, as we are still friends, we will run together to your rendezvous."

As the two young men pressed on through the hours of the early night, the storm broke in waves upon them. Soaked to the bone, they emerged from the forest track onto the lakeshore. Tumultuous clouds obscured the moon, but through the torrents of rain, they could make out the white-capped waves lashing the shoreline. Barnabas wondered how even a pistol shot could be heard above the clamor of thunder and cracks of lightning. Passage on such a night seemed impossible. They retreated into the shelter of the forest as Barnabas searched for his cache of clothes. He nearly fell over the rocky crevice in which he had stuffed the bundle a month ago. He knew now that he was in the right place at the right time. When the worst of the storm abated, he carefully withdrew the pistol from under his hunting shirt and primed it with powder that he prayed was still dry enough to ignite.

When the moon finally fought free from the thick clouds, he stepped into the open and fired the pistol into the air. Its report was satisfyingly sharp. Then he rejoined Squando to wait within the tree line for the arrival of the promised boat. After minutes that seemed very long, a hoarse voice called into the wind the words of the message Sergeant Joshua had first whispered into his ear at Green's Crossing. "Audemus jura nostra defendere." "We dare to defend our rights," words in Latin only Barnabas would recognize. He breathed a sigh of relief. Only expected parties had arrived at the rendezvous.

He turned to Squando to make his farewells. But Squando was already gone. Barnabas smiled. "I hope he gets that good night's sleep."

Sergeant Joshua hustled him into a boat manned by four seasoned oarsmen. Barnabas added little weight to the cargo. His body slumping in exhaustion, he gave up the burden of his mission into the capable hands of Sergeant Joshua. He felt himself wrapped like a package into a length of canvas, protection from flying spray as the boat skimmed across the narrows. His next impression was of being carried out of the boat and into the fort. After that, he plunged into a deep and dreamless sleep and did not awake until his shoulder was firmly shaken. The first light of day was creeping up the stone walls.

"Thank God," he said. It was Ned's face peering into his own, a bandage wrapped around his head. "Not dead after all." He would have fallen back into sleep, but Ned shook him harder.

"Wake up! They need to talk to you, Barny." Ned raised his cousin against the pillow and held a cup of cold water to his lips. Then, he turned to address other figures in the room. "Now, Sirs. He's ready to speak." And Ned retreated to the other end of the room.

Barnabas realized that he had awakened in a narrow bunk at the far end of the dispensary. He looked about, still in the fog of sleep, but pulled himself alert when he recognized Captain Whitcomb and the familiar figure of Quartermaster Udney Hay.

"At ease, Corporal," the captain said, laying a hand on Barnabas's shoulder. He and the quartermaster drew up stools beside the bed. The captain put the knotted cords of yarn into Barnabas's hands. "Explain these." To Ned, he said, "You, Corporal Locke, take down what your cousin tells us." The captain produced a campaign writing desk containing all the required implements. Ned approached and seated himself at the small table the quartermaster pulled close to the bed. He withdrew paper and ink, a slight tremor in his right hand.

As Barnabas began to explain his cipher by knots and colors, the captain nodded in approval. "An old rangers' trick. I lay odds taught you by your father." A grueling hour of questions, mostly addressed to him by the captain, ensued. With each length of yarn accounted for, Barnabas felt lightened of his burden of information.

"Now, explain how this ledger and this letter came into your possession," the quartermaster demanded, tapping the ledger where it lay on the table.

"I took them from Private George Crawley. He was a traitor. It was him who revealed my name and mission to the British, who put a bounty on my head. It was him who knocked out Ned—I mean Corporal Locke—with intent to kill. It was him who stole the book and the letter. George Crawley told me so himself."

"And where is this Private George Crawley?"

"Dead under a pine tree." Suddenly, Barnabas felt a great exhaustion. His face whitened. He had looked into Georgie's face as he died, and it left a bitter memory.

Captain Whitcomb briefly patted his shoulder. Cheerfully, he said, "The British intend to hang me, too, and they've got more reason."

When the quartermaster signaled they were done, Ned affixed his signature as the scribe with a shaking hand and raised with relief his quill from the last sheet of the report. He presented the signature page to all parties, noting that Barnabas gripped the quill to steady his hand. He then carefully blotted and assembled the pages, handing the report to Quartermaster Hay.

Captain Whitcomb leaned over to shake Barnabas by the hand. "Well done, Corporal. Now rest, and we will talk again later." The quartermaster echoed the captain's "Well done," and the two rose to depart.

"One question, Sir, if I may. Why do you address me as corporal?"

The captain turned back and said, "You were a corporal the night you left on this mission."

When the two cousins were alone together, Barnabas raised his hand, as Squando did, to signify a serious conversation. He beckoned his cousin closer and recited to him, word for word and almost with his aunt's cadences, the message she had entrusted to him for her son. Then, with a ragged breath, he addressed Ned. "Will you grant me a very large favor, Ned? I will understand should you say no." Ned replied, "Spit it out, Barny."

"Before Georgie Crawley died, he made a request of me. To send word to his father that he had died loyal to his oath. His father should know that his son has died and where his body lies. Will you help me write that letter, Ned, and send it to his family in Boston?"

Ned blew out the candles on the little table. He sighed deeply and climbed shakily back into his bunk. In a short while, his low voice answered Barnabas. "Yes, Barny, I'll help write that letter. I'll do that much for us both." Sleep overtook the cousins.

Late that afternoon, while Barnabas was wolfing down his share and most of Ned's of the generous meal brought by an orderly, their conversation was halted by Sergeant Joshua's arrival. He greeted the two corporals jovially but sat down heavily on one of the stools at the table.

"I trust you lads are in good enough shape to move out. Other scouts have been returning from the western shore with reports that confirm your own. Gentleman Johnny is sailing down the lake and will be above us at Fort Crown Point in a matter of days. That may delay them from our gates for a short while. The powers that be are wrestling now about how to defend this fort, undermanned as it is, from a force near four times greater. It's a bloody great Armada bearing down on us. Mount Defiance, that great lump of unfortified rock," and the sergeant nodded dismissively in that direction, "that's the Achilles' heel in our defenses. Better to retreat and fight another day, I say. This fort will be evacuated—the wounded and sick first, and that's you, laddies. The captain is marching his Rangers to Albany. We three are Whitcomb's men, and I expect to see you both in Albany ready to fight when next we meet."

It was a long speech from the normally taciturn sergeant. The cousins recognized that he was putting as good a face as he could paint on a bitter situation. Barnabas felt a pang of personal defeat as though his efforts had been for naught. Ned's cooler head, though sorely aching, saw at once the wisdom of retreat.

Barnabas, remembering the pistol he still carried in Georgie's haversack, said, "Sergeant, the pistol you lent me. I want to return it to you with my thanks. I only fired it that once on the lakeshore. But I stood down a Hessian with it and held it against a traitor to boot."

Sergeant Joshua chuckled. "That German pistol has stood me in good stead these many years. Since I was a smuggler in my misbegotten youth. Hold on to it, lad. Maybe you'll capture a British general with it yet."

Two days after the Locke cousins were evacuated from Ticonderoga with other sick and injured soldiers, the entire garrison of over two thousand men slipped away in the middle of the night between the fifth and sixth of July. Even as the Americans retreated, General Burgoyne's forces were hauling cannon up the facing flanks of undefended Mount Defiance.

Soon after regrouping in Albany, Barnabas privately urged Sergeant Joshua to recommend Ned for convalescent leave. Georgie's hammer blow to Ned's head had left him unsteady and unfit. Headache, tremors and blurry vision plagued him. Ned tried to hide the extent of his injuries, but it was clear to Barnabas and Sergeant Joshua that he must recover at home rather than in sick quarters, where dysentery carried off healthier young men than Ned.

When the order came through, Ned was furious and sharp enough to detect Barnabas's influence in the decision. "How could you conspire against me, Barny? All I need is time to recuperate. I'll be fine!" Ned felt, to his secret shame, that a skunk like Georgie Crawley had bested him and escaped with the essential ledger on his watch. He wanted desperately to redeem himself in his own eyes.

"You can recuperate better at home," Barnabas retorted coldly. Selfishly, as he admitted to himself, he wanted to return to his duties free of responsibility for his cousin. He wanted Ned safely under the care of Aunt Elizabeth with the dog Stringer standing guard.

"I know this war was to be the great adventure of your life, Ned. But being dead is no adventure." Soon after, the cousins parted with affection, but without the warm camaraderie as on that day they enlisted at Green's Crossing. Ned was traveling north on a medical wagon, and Barnabas north with Whitcomb's Rangers to a place called Freeman's Farm, twenty miles north of Albany near Saratoga.

SEVEN

A BRAVE HORSE

Barnabas sat astride his bay horse in the late afternoon of October 7, 1777, intently watching the flaps of General Benedict Arnold's tent at army headquarters. Upon their arrival at Freeman's Farm in early September, Captain Whitcomb had assigned him as a courier to General Arnold. Again serving as his captain's eyes and ears, Barnabas kept him informed as the ongoing feud intensified between the commanding General Horatio Gates and his second-in-command General Arnold.

Barnabas had paid a seamstress, one of many camp followers, to stitch a corporal's green epaulet onto his coat's right shoulder and a chevron stripe on his left upper arm. He requested, as his usual mount, the fast little bay gelding he had ridden through deep woods on his enlistment day. As necessary, he and Little Bay together delivered orders and messages between the lines of engagement, often under fire.

Earlier on this October day, Barnabas had accompanied General Arnold on a reconnoiter, revealing that Burgoyne's forces were moving strongly on the left of the American position. There had been constant heated exchanges throughout the day between the daring, hot-tempered Arnold and his superior, the jealous, ambitious but cautious General Gates. Barnabas gathered that Gates had just dismissed his second-in-command from the field of battle. Arnold, Barnabas knew, was seething within the tent he was watching.

Since the ill-fated pursuit of the retreating Continental Army from Fort Ticonderoga, Burgoyne's forces had marched miles through swampy woodland while Major Daniel Morgan's famed sharpshooters picked off his officers. Promised reinforcements never arrived. British strength, morale and rations had steadily ebbed. The dashing "Gentleman Johnny" no longer seemed invincible.

On the nineteenth of September, the two armies finally clashed at Freeman's Farm. That bloody day ended in stalemate, although General Arnold had distinguished himself on the field to the fury of his commanding officer. Afterward, the opposing armies regrouped with the forces of General Gates strategically entrenched on Beamis Heights above the wide, stump-filled fields of Freeman's Farm. The British, with their Hessian artillerists, threw up two massive redoubts from which to direct cannon fire. After days of constant skirmishing between pickets and patrols, Burgoyne had finally mounted a desperate second attempt to wrest victory from a steadily deteriorating position.

Throughout the day, Barnabas had heard cannons and gunfire, signifying that the two armies had engaged. A fine horse, saddled for action, stood tethered outside Arnold's tent. Barnabas was ready to follow the general at an instant's notice. When Arnold stormed from his tent, mounted the waiting horse in one swift motion, and galloped toward the front, Barnabas kicked Little Bay into immediate pursuit. His eyes remained fixed on the general's blue coat, his epaulet a spill of gold over his left shoulder. That flash of gold triggered a sudden vision of a glint of gold on a rocky ledge when he left Fort Ticonderoga on his clandestine mission. Barnabas angrily shook the image from his mind.

Within moments, Arnold caught up with a fresh brigade of Connecticut militiamen, who cheered their own native son and local hero, falling into line behind him. When Arnold galloped into the heart of the battle, the British had fallen back to the protection of the two redoubts, from which they directed a storm of hot lead. Ignoring the whistle of musket balls and grapeshot, Barnabas focussed only on the general's back. One shot grazed Little Bay on his rump. He stumbled but steadied. The fire of artillery deafened Barnabas, and acrid smoke stung his eyes. The wounded groaned about him. Fallen horses screamed. Only the dead were silent. As the militia advanced and then faltered under withering fire between the two British redoubts, Barnabas momentarily lost sight of the general.

When he next spied him, Arnold was riding with reckless disregard in the open between the two British redoubts, under fire and waving his sword in the air like a madman. Barnabas thought it the bravest act of leadership an officer could perform. Taking instant advantage of an opening between the redoubts, Arnold led a furious charge, turning his Connecticut forces headlong into one redoubt's unprotected left flank. As the German artillerists abandoned their guns and ran, Arnold's fine horse was hit in a last volley. To his horror, Barnabas saw horse and rider fall as one. He urged Little Bay forward and leaped to the ground at the side of the thrashing horse. Arnold's left leg had taken a bullet, was bleeding copiously and was pinned beneath his horse.

Barnabas seized the bridle of the stricken animal, stroking its starred face and murmuring a soft stream of soothing words. Arnold was alert; pain had not yet overtaken him. In a calm voice, he said, "Save this brave horse, Corporal. He has been faithful to me." Tugging on the bridle, Barnabas encouraged the horse to rise and with a heave, the animal collected his shaky legs under him and rose. Even in distress, he avoided stepping on the man beneath him. Already, Arnold's fellow militiamen had hurried to the aid of their fallen general. A fast runner was sent to alert the surgeon and to summon a litter.

Barnabas hastily examined the horse's wound and thought it would not prove fatal. Keeping the reins of the injured horse firmly in his hand, Barnabas remounted Little Bay, standing by patiently. Among sporadic musket fire, the three of them followed the litter as Arnold was carried to the surgeon's tent. When the general, now in agony, was borne away, Barnabas inquired where to find the horse surgeon. He was directed to a makeshift corral, far in the back of the encampment, where a kindly man took the reins from him, recognizing the limping bloodied horse at once. His brows lifted in inquiry.

Barnabas replied to the inquisitive eyebrows, "Yes, this is General Arnold's horse. Both fell wounded in battle, but I believe they will survive their wounds. Do you have an ointment to soothe this graze on my own brave horse?"

EIGHT

HOW EVENTS PLAY OUT

A chill October wind whipped the American flag over a large white tent on a hilltop overlooking the Hudson River just outside the village of Saratoga. Barnabas, astride Little Bay, was on courier duty and, though apart from the officers, had a good view of the ranks of soldiers below—American troops guarding six thousand disarmed British soldiers, German mercenaries, and Loyalists—to a man hungry, cold and dispirited. Among them, Barnabas searched for a certain foppish British lieutenant but saw no sign of Pendleton. "Probably sulking in a tent somewhere," he muttered to himself.

But nothing could spoil the glory of this day when Lieutenant General "Gentleman Johnny" Burgoyne surrendered to Major General Horatio Gates after a miserable retreat from Freeman's Farm. He and his soundly thrashed army had sworn to depart American soil forever. Barnabas frowned when General Gates declined acceptance of Gentleman Johnny's sword. Instead, the general genially ushered Burgoyne and his officers into the tent for refreshments. "They're a class far above us, Little Bay," he opined, stroking the glossy bay neck before him.

His spirits rose again when prompted by fifes and drums striking up a lively marching air; the American soldiers burst spontaneously into the derisive British song they had adopted as their own. Barnabas laughed aloud and sang along lustily, "Yankee Doodle came to town, a'riding on a pony. He stuck a feather in his hat and called it Macaroni." And then the chorus, even louder, "Yankee Doodle, keep it up, Yankee Doodle Dandy, mind the music and the step and with the girls be handy."

Three days later, thanks to leave as promised by Sergeant Joshua, he sang the song again over supper in the warm kitchen of the Locke Farm with his aunt and uncle and cousins merrily joining in. "Mark my words; the lobster backs have lost this war. Just you wait until the French come into it on our side," his Uncle Edward said. He was a man taking the pulse of his own country as it came into being.

After the washing up and Enoch and Sally, under protest, were sent to bed, Barnabas handed his uncle a sealed letter put into his own hands by Deputy Quartermaster General Udney Hay.

His uncle whistled after he had read the missive. "The army is offering me a contract for provisions through to the end of this war. Wants me to persuade the farmers and tradesmen hereabouts to sign onto these government contracts for everything from apples to lumber. Well, we are patriots, but we have to make a living the same as everyone else and our new government," and he emphasized the word "government," "is flat busted. We can't get by on scrip with nothing behind it. The high and mighty plan to buy off officers and enlisted men with land deeds to land they don't even own. How will they pay us?" Ned and his father leaned their heads together as they debated the merits of accepting or refusing the offer. Aunt Elizabeth listened attentively as she darned, Stringer dozing at her feet. Barnabas said little, gladly watching his cousin Ned, medically discharged from the army, animated and already figuring out costs. "He's near himself again," he thought. "And wearing spectacles somehow suits him."

In April 1779, Barnabas re-enlisted for another two years under now Major Benjamin Whitcomb's Rangers, remaining in the upper region of the northeast territories. As the war moved south, the Rangers checked British incursions from Canada and engaged in raids and scouting expeditions into enemy territory. Through their own good intelligence gathering, they thwarted a British secret expedition to burn mills and supply sources. Barnabas and Little Bay found themselves in some tight spots, more often than not saved by Little Bay's alert and quick responses. Though these adventures might have ended in capture or death, they did make for good tales to share in the Locke kitchen, like a price he willingly paid for family warmth and hearty food.

On leave with yet another sealed letter in his courier bag, he was greeted at the barn by his old friend Zeke and his Abenaki bride Molly. Molly's people were packing up to go into the Ohio Country. She was the daughter of a line of peacemakers who had handed down the same English name for generations. Honored women, they advised the elders in Abenaki councils. Those council fires were being extinguished.

Molly looked Barnabas in the eye as she repeated to him, faithfully word for word and falling unconsciously into the cadences of her brother's voice, a message from Squando.

Greetings to my friend and brother, Barnabas Locke. My sister Molly is now Zeke's wife by our traditions. Many of us are going into the Ohio Country. There, we have the promise of welcome and lands to hunt with our brethren to the west. When I dream of you, I see us together in wide grassy places open to the sky. Keep well. We will meet again.

Farming in his bones, Zeke was desperate for acres to call his own. As white settlers swarmed into Vermont, displacing Molly's people, farmland had grown scarce. With no intention of ever being a farmer himself, Barnabas sold Zeke his inheritance; the small farm had long fallen into neglect and disrepair since the death of Frederick Locke. His terms were generous, sweetened by Molly's promise of a new pair of elk skin moccasins every year they lived on the farm.

Sometimes, he found himself teasing Ned, a dangerous thing to do. "She's mighty pretty and smart and thinks high of herself. She won't stay long on the vine, so maybe you better ask Miss Lucy Forester to say 'yes.'" Ned threw the apple or the account book or the mug or whatever was at hand in sharp reply. Thanks be, never his tomahawk, still carried in his belt. Secretly, Barnabas thought Ned was too embroiled in the heated local politicking around the move to establish an independent State of Vermont. His brief military career spent in the quartermaster's office and his current dealings in army contracts were already assets to his budding political ambitions. A wife like Miss Lucy Forester, who had ambitions of her own, would suit him well, his cousin thought.

In December 1780, Barnabas arrived distraught at the Locke Farm. The news had come before him, and his aunt and uncle greeted him somberly. "There's folks around here who just can't believe it," Uncle Edward said, shaking his head in disbelief. Dismay and outrage over the discovery of General Benedict Arnold's treason swept the country. "How," Barnabas wondered bitterly, "could such a brave man do such a cowardly deed?" He thought again of Georgie Crawley's claim that he, too, was a patriot to his Loyalist cause. But Benedict Arnold had put personal gain and his grievances above his country's interests. Even Georgie Crawley had not sunk that low.

Barnabas fell into long spells of hard thought. At twenty-one, he was eager to get on with the life he wanted—a life in the wilderness, the life of a frontiersman beholden to no one. He pondered Sergeant Joshua's advice, "Better to get out ahead of the rest. Clever young fellows like you can make their fortune in land for sure."

One morning, as the end of his second enlistment drew near, Barnabas was bid by Sergeant Joshua to report to Quartermaster Hay. He left that meeting with a sealed letter of introduction, particular instructions, and enough silver coin to buy two packhorses and trade goods to make himself welcome wherever he went. He also had a government receipt for the purchase of one bay gelding, sound of limb, seven years old and nearly fifteen hands high at the withers. Like his good friend Squando, he and Little Bay were bound for the Ohio Country.

TO BE CONTINUED

About the Author

MATTHEW BLAINE enjoys swapping stories with interesting people with their own stories to tell, especially around campfires. Although his education was hampered by dyslexia, he got another sort of education in the company of Ernest Hemingway, Jack London, Louis L'Amour, John Steinbeck and, when he could get them, men's adventure magazines. After stints as a cab driver, steelworker, factory floor assembler and carpenter, he worked for thirty years managing trade shows on the East Coast. During the pandemic, he wrote two self-printed memoirs about his travel and outdoor adventures. That triggered an ambition to write honest fiction in which he could reinvent himself in the lives of historical fictional characters. An avid primitive archer, canoeist, long-distance hiker, minimalist, and unionist, Matthew travels with an eye for the obscure stories of the past.

Retired, he lives in a rural Pennsylvania county, haunting flea markets for goods to trade with fellow outdoorsmen at swaps and archery rendezvous. In a little shop inside his woods, he practices the skills required for leather working, shaping and fletching primitive arrows, and marrying old axeheads with newly-fashioned handles.